Puppy Friends #2

Lily the Lost Puppy

by Jenny Dale

Illustrated by Frank Rodgers

D1473700

Aladdin Paperbacks

Look for these Puppy Friends books!

#1 Gus the Greedy Puppy
#2 Lily the Lost Puppy

Coming soon

#3 Spot the Sporty Puppy
#4 Lenny the Lazy Puppy

First Aladdin Paperbacks edition January 2000

Text copyright © 1999 by Working Partners Limited
Illustrations copyright © 1999 by Frank Rodgers
Activity Fun Pages text copyright © 2000 by Stasia Ward Kehoe
First published 1999 by Macmillan Children's Books U.K.
Created by Working Partners Limited

Aladdin Paperbacks
An imprint of Simon & Schuster
Children's Publishing Division
1230 Avenue of the Americas
New York, NY 10020

The text for this book was set in Palatino.
Printed and bound in the United States of America
6 8 10 9 7 5

Library of Congress Catalog Card Number: 99-67695
ISBN 0-689-83404-7

Chapter One

"Lily! Watch out!" Jack was dragging an empty suitcase across his bedroom floor, right past where Lily was sniffing a really interesting patch of bare floorboard. It was full of new smells because the rug had been taken up only the day before.

Hmm, thought Lily, as her small black nose snuffled along the floor. *Just the faintest whiff of mouse. And something else—old cookie crumbs, maybe?*

"Lily, move!" Jack called out again.

"OKAY, OKAY! I'm moving!" Lily yapped as she skipped out of the way. Wherever she was, Lily seemed to be in the wrong place.

During the last few days, the whole family seemed to have gone crazy! There were boxes all over the house and everyone was making a huge fuss about packing things into them. Even Jack had been behaving oddly—he'd hardly played with her for ages. And he was supposed to be her best friend!

Lily lay down with her head between her paws. Why was everyone packing

2

their things away? Was it some sort of game? No, it couldn't be, because when Lily had started playing in all that great newspaper lying on the hall floor yesterday, she'd gotten into trouble.

Jack packed the last of his clothes into a suitcase and tried to shut the lid. He'd put far too many things in it. Lily watched as Jack bounced up and down on the suitcase, trying to get the two edges to meet. After a lot of hard work, he managed to get the lid closed at last and clicked the two clasps together.

"*Now* can we play?" yapped Lily, sitting up and cocking her head to one side.

Jack understood. "Okay, Lil, we'll go and play in a minute," he replied. "I've just got one more thing to do first."

Lily slumped back down again, then spotted a shoelace hanging out of the suitcase. She trotted over and sniffed it. *Great!* she thought. *I'd know that shoelace anywhere. It belongs to one of the cleats Jack uses for soccer.* She grabbed the shoelace and started tugging.

"Hey, stop it, Lil!" cried Jack.

But Lily carried on. She tugged and tugged, and suddenly the lid of the suitcase burst open. Lily yipped in delight. This was more like it! She picked up the shoe in her teeth and shook it playfully.

"Drop it, Lily!" said Jack sternly. "That's one of my best cleats."

"No way," growled Lily. "It's one of your smelliest."

Jack made a grab for the shoe, but Lily held on, and won. She raced out of the bedroom and downstairs, with the cleat still clamped firmly in her mouth. Jack clattered down after her.

As they raced along the hall, Mr. Harper, Jack's father, came out of the living room. "I hope you've finished your packing, Jack," he called. "The moving guys will be here any minute."

Lily skidded across the kitchen floor and made for the dog door in the back door. But the square opening of the dog door wasn't wide enough for Lily *and* Jack's soccer cleat. Lily bounced back and landed in a heap.

"Aha! Gotcha!" cried Jack as he caught up with Lily and grabbed the shoe away from her. She then shot through the dog door and into the backyard. Jack opened the door and raced after her.

They followed their usual marathon route across the small lawn: around the fishpond—twice both ways, around the birch tree, across to the vegetable patch and back down the other side. . . .

Then Lily stopped in her tracks as she heard a deep rumbling sound from the street.

"That's the truck coming to take everything away!" cried Jack.

"What?" yelped Lily. She cocked her head at Jack. "Why would they want to do that?"

"Come on, Lil, we're moving to a new house," Jack explained. "It's got a huge backyard. We'll have a great time there!"

Lily felt cold all over. Her stumpy little tail drooped in protest. "But I don't want to go!" she growled. "I like it here!"

Jack took no notice and raced back to the house. Lily followed, feeling very upset.

She didn't want to move to a strange new house. She had friends around here. There was Bruce the Labrador at Number 10. And Wendy the terrier, who lived around the corner. They met every day in the park. Lily hadn't even said goodbye to them!

The house was now full of men in overalls clumping all over the place. They were shouting to each other in loud voices and carrying all the furniture out of the house. Mrs. Harper, Jack's mom, was fussing around, telling them to be careful.

Lily peered out of the front door and watched the men putting furniture into a huge truck that was waiting outside in the road with its back doors open. It was all too much for Lily. She started shivering with fright.

Jack noticed and held out his arms. "Here, Lil!" he called. She leaped gratefully into his arms and snuggled against his chest.

"Exciting, isn't it?" said Jack, ruffling the wiry white fur of Lily's neck.

Lily watched as the kitchen table was carried through the front door. "*I* don't think so!" she whined back. "I think it's *scary!*"

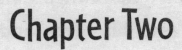

Chapter Two

When all the rolled-up carpets and furniture had gone, the men started to carry boxes outside to the truck. Mr. Harper came out of the kitchen with Lily's basket. "Maybe Lily should come with me," he told Jack's mom. "There's more room in my car for her basket." He started taking the basket outside.

"Hey! Where are you going with that?" barked Lily.

"Don't worry, Lily, all your toys are in there!" said Mr. Harper, smiling as he walked toward the front door. "Come on then!" he called to her over his shoulder.

Jack put Lily down. "Go with Dad, Lil," he said. "I'm just going to say good-bye to my bedroom."

Lily hesitated—she'd have much rather stayed with Jack—then trotted outside after Mr. Harper. He put her basket on the back seat of his large car, which was parked in front of Mrs. Harper's smaller red one. Then he nodded toward the open car door. "Okay, Lily. Get in," he said.

Lily reluctantly jumped in and Mr. Harper slammed the door shut. Lily circled around in her basket a few times, nudging the blanket to get her bed the way she liked it. Just then, there was a loud crunch as one of the men hit something hard against the truck.

"Hey! Careful with that!" Mr. Harper called out, and went over to see if anything had been damaged.

Lily whined unhappily. She hated being on her own, and everything was suddenly so strange and frightening. She wanted to be with Jack.

Then Lily noticed that one of the front doors of the car wasn't quite shut. She leaped out of her basket, into the front seat, and slipped out through the gap.

Back in the house, Jack was nowhere to be seen. *Maybe he's still in his bedroom,* Lily thought. She trotted upstairs, her claws clicking on the bare wooden floorboards. But there was no sign of him.

Lily hung around, having a few final sniffs in the corners of the room before continuing her search.

Then suddenly, something terrible happened. Jack's bedroom door slammed shut. Someone had shut Lily in!

Lily was so surprised she didn't do anything at first. She heard someone shutting the other bedroom doors, and the heavy front door slammed shut. Then the roaring engine of the moving truck started up. She couldn't believe it. Surely they weren't going without her?

Lily rushed over and scratched furiously at the bottom of the bedroom door, but it was shut tight. She leaped up at the door handle and caught at it with her paw, but the door stayed closed. She began to bark and bark like mad, but the truck was making so much noise outside, nobody could hear her.

Lily heard Mr. Harper's car engine start up. She ran over to the window. But even when she stood up on her hind legs, she was too short to reach the windowsill.

"See you there!" she heard Mr. Harper shout out as the truck doors clanged shut.

"Okay!" Mrs. Harper shouted back. Lily heard Mr. Harper's car slowly driving away.

Very faintly, over the noise of the moving truck, Jack's voice came floating up to Lily. "Lily did go with Dad, didn't she?"

Lily's ears pricked up. "No, I didn't!" she barked. "I'm here!" She scrabbled a bit more under the windowsill, trying desperately to reach it.

"Yes, I saw her get in the car," Lily heard Jack's mom reply. "She'll be there waiting for you at the new house."

Lily's heart pounded with fear and panic, thumping painfully against her chest. "No!" she barked. "Don't go without me!"

"Hey!" she heard Jack say. "That sounded like Lily!"

"It can't be," his mom replied. "She went with Dad. I told you—I saw her get in the car."

Lily took a deep breath and leaped as

high as she could above the windowsill,
hoping that Jack would see her. But she
couldn't stay up in the air, and he didn't
look up at the right time.

Lily's brown, pointed ears twitched as
she listened to the doors of Mrs.
Harper's red car slamming shut. The
engine started up and the car pulled

slowly away, following the rumbling moving truck. Lily heard the car make the crunching noise it always made when it was going around corners. It must have been turning onto the avenue where she and Jack walked to the park.

The sound of the engine slowly faded away, then disappeared completely. Lily was alone.

Lily stayed at the window for a while, listening for the sound of the car to return. Surely they would come back for her? But the street remained silent. She began to whimper. Her white furry body quivered with shock.

Then, suddenly, a little spark of courage lit up inside her. "Come on! Be brave!" she told herself.

She stood up and shook herself, then circled the room trying to think what to do next.

She looked at the door. Maybe if she tried really hard she could jump up high enough to reach the door handle with her paw. Then she could get out of the house, run down the street, and catch up with Jack.

Yes!

Lily went over and started to leap up at the door handle. At first she kept missing. But she kept on, jumping again and again on her short, strong legs. At last, she caught the handle with her front paws. It jerked down as Lily fell back, and the catch gave way. The door swung open. She'd done it!

Lily pushed the door open farther with her nose. In a flash, she was out of the room and streaking down the stairs. She skidded across the bare floorboards of the hallway toward the kitchen and . . .

. . . slammed straight into the closed kitchen door. For the second time that day, Lily landed in a heap. The door was shut tight, and the handle was much higher than the one in Jack's bedroom. Lily would never be able to reach it. All was lost!

She slumped miserably against the door and let out of a howl of despair.

Then Lily heard the sound of a car engine outside. Doors slammed. She heard voices and footsteps coming up the front path. Jack had missed her after all, and had come back for her.

Hooray!

Lily ran to the front door, her little stump of a tail wagging so hard she thought it would fall off.

She heard the rattle of keys.

"*Woof!*" she barked happily. "I'm still here!"

"What was that?" said a woman's voice.

"What does Mrs. Harper mean?" wondered Lily. "Surely she knows it's me!"

The keys rattled a bit more, then the front door swung open. But the people standing in the doorway weren't Lily's family.

Chapter Three

"Goodness!" said the lady who wasn't Mrs. Harper. "What are you doing here?"

Lily's heart sank as she looked up at the strangers. "What are *you* doing here?" she barked. "I wanted it to be Jack!" Lily's mind raced. She didn't want to stay here! There was only one thing to do.

Lily shot out of the front door past the

strange family, down the path and out of the gate. She ran down the street, heading in the direction in which she'd heard Mrs. Harper's red car going.

"Hey! Where are you going?" barked Bruce through the gate at Number 10.

"Sorry, can't stop!" woofed Lily breathlessly over her shoulder. "I've got to find Jack!"

Lily raced around the corner into the road lined with trees. She knew it like the back of her paw—it led to the big noisy road at the end, with the park on the other side, where she and Jack went for walks. Without even stopping to sniff at lampposts she ran on, with the wind rushing past her ears.

At the corner, Lily skidded to a halt. How would she know which way the red car had turned next? She growled in despair, looking up and down the road.

In the doorway of the corner shop she spotted Yeoman, the old sheepdog who lived there. *He might have seen which way the car went,* thought Lily. She trotted eagerly up to him.

"What are you doing out on your own, Lily?" he asked.

"Something terrible has happened," she whined. My family has gone to live somewhere else and left me behind by mistake!"

"Oh no!" Yeoman replied. "Don't you think you'd better go back and wait for them? They're bound to come back for you."

"*No!*" yelped Lily. "Some strange people have arrived at the house!" She asked Yeoman if he'd seen Mrs. Harper's red car, but he hadn't.

"But Wendy might have seen the car," Yeoman suggested. "She sees everything on this street! She just went to the park with her owner."

"I'd better go and find her," Lily said. She trotted briskly to the main road.

A loud motorcycle sped past, making Lily jump. Her brown eyes opened wide with fright. She cowered on the pavement for a while. The traffic seemed even noisier and faster than usual. She'd never tried to cross a road on her own before. If only she was here with Jack and on her leash.

Then Lily noticed the black and white stripes on the road, where she and Jack usually crossed. The traffic had stopped there and people were walking across, so Lily followed, lost among a sea of legs.

As soon as she reached the other side, Lily darted through the park gates. She looked around, searching for Wendy, but there was no sign of her.

Lily trotted over to the pond, where she and Jack used to have such fun feeding the ducks. Her tail drooped sadly. "Oh, where *is* he?" she howled.

At that moment, Jack was slumped miserably on the stairs at the new house. "I *did* hear Lily barking in the old house!" he wailed at his parents. "And now she's run off and I might never see her again!" His shoulders heaved with sobs.

The Harpers had arrived at the new house and discovered the terrible mistake. Mr. Harper had thought Lily was still in his car when he'd driven off. After all, he hadn't seen her get out. But when Mrs.

Harper phoned the old house, the new family had told her they'd seen Lily—and she'd run off!

"We have to go and look for her right away!" Jack cried.

"Okay," his mom agreed. "Let's go. Dad can stay here and start the unpacking."

Back in the park, Lily sat by the pond, her small body shivering despite the sunshine.

"Hey! What's the matter?"

Lily looked up. It was Wendy, the terrier, coming toward her, wagging her long feathery tail. Wendy's owner was sitting on a bench nearby.

"What are you doing out here on your own?" Wendy asked.

Lily told her the whole sad story and asked if Wendy had seen Jack go past in his mom's red car.

Wendy tilted her head to one side and thought hard. "Well," she began slowly, "there are quite a lot of red cars around . . . but wait a minute!" She yelped excitedly.

"Yes, I do remember! It turned onto the main road, and went—that way!" Wendy turned her head to point out the direction. "But I'd take the shortcut through the park if I were you," she advised wisely. "Better than going back onto that busy main road."

"Thanks, Wendy!" said Lily gratefully. She ran off in the direction Wendy had pointed.

Lily ran and ran, coming to a part of the park where she and Jack had never been. She slowed down and looked around, panting.

It was all very different here. The stores outside the railings seemed fancier, and the houses and yards were bigger.

Lily was very thirsty. She found a small puddle and drank greedily from it. *Yuck!* It tasted horrible. She spat it out.

"Those dogs from the other side of the park have such dreadful manners!"

Lily turned around and saw two large, snooty-looking dogs with lots of silky hair that fell around them like curtains. They were pulling their owners along on two long, stretchy leashes. They came toward Lily and began sniffing her in a most unfriendly way. Lily noticed they had very fancy collars on.

"Oh dear, what kind of scruffy pup is this?" said one.

"And what kind of owner lets such a youngster run loose in the park?" sniffed the other. "Honestly! Some humans!"

The two tall dogs towered over Lily, looking down their long thin noses at her.

Lily's legs stiffened and the wiry hair on her back bristled angrily. They were being rude about Jack! She was about to tell the snooty dogs just what she thought of them when a familiar noise made Lily prick up her ears. It was the crunching sound of Mrs. Harper's car engine.

"Excuse me!" she barked, and ran out from behind the two dogs—just in time to see Jack's mom's red car driving past.

Lily yelped with excitement and dashed out through the park gates after the car. She raced down the pavement, dodging people's legs. She just had to catch up with it! Without looking, she galloped out onto the road, then heard a roaring sound, getting louder and louder—and closer. Lily looked up and saw a big red bus heading right toward her!

Chapter Four

Lily cowered, frozen in terror. Then she realized that the bus had slowed down. Luckily for Lily, it was stopping to let passengers on and off.

Lily crept back onto the pavement and watched as the bus slowly pulled away again. There was no sign of the red car now. She whined miserably.

Suddenly, a strange rumbling noise came from Lily's tummy. She realized she was very hungry! *I might as well go and find something to eat,* she thought.

With a heavy heart, Lily got up and trotted off down the street, sniffing the air for smells of food.

A couple of streets away, Jack and his mom had stopped the car. They were talking to a lady who was being dragged along by the two snooty dogs who had been rude to Lily.

"Have you seen a Jack Russell puppy who looks lost?" Jack asked.

The lady thought for a moment, then smiled. "Yes," she replied. "Not long ago, in the park. Perdita and Polly went up to her, then she ran out through the park gates."

"It must have been Lily!" cried Jack excitedly.

"Did you see which direction she went?" Mrs. Harper asked.

The lady shook her head.

Jack's shoulders drooped. "She could have gone anywhere!" he said miserably.

Jack's mom thanked the lady and turned to comfort him. "We'll just keep on looking," she said. "Lily can't be very far away!"

Lily wandered farther and farther in her search for food. She didn't recognize this street at all. She passed a house with a delicious smell of cooking coming from it and pushed her nose through the gate.

"Rarrghhh! Rarrghhh!"

Lily leapt backward in fright as a huge pair of snarling jaws appeared from nowhere. They belonged to an

enormous black dog who loomed above her in a very scary way.

"Scram, pup! This is my yard!" he snapped.

Lily didn't hang around. She turned tail and ran and ran until she came to an alleyway lined with garbage cans and big black bags. Food!

She started nosing around the bags. When she found one that smelled promising, she tore it open with her sharp white teeth.

Inside, she found a stale crust of bread and the remains of a hamburger, which she gulped down hungrily.

"You can tell this one hasn't been on the streets for long!"

Lily turned to see a pair of scruffy mutts staring at her. They looked a bit rough, but they were wagging their tails in a friendly way.

"Oh, pardon me," woofed Lily politely. "Is this your yard?"

The two mutts wagged their tails harder. "We don't believe in that kind of thing," said one. "We strays range far and wide! We hunt in groups and share everything!"

"So what's your story, little one?" asked the other stray. "Have you been away from home long?"

Lily poured out the whole sorry story. The two mutts listened, cocking their heads sympathetically.

"Don't worry," said one of them, when Lily had finished. "You're not alone anymore. My name's Sam and this is Shep. We'll look after you. Come with us and we'll find you a delicious meal!"

Lily followed her two new friends through a maze of narrow side streets and alleyways until they came to a courtyard full of garbage cans. They smelled strongly of all kinds of delicious food.

"Here we are!" announced Sam proudly. "The back of Marcello's restaurant. Best food in town!"

In no time, Sam and Shep had raided the garbage cans and brought out a variety of tasty leftovers. There was steak and chicken, with crunchy cookies

for dessert. They all dived in greedily.

"Well!" woofed Sam, when they'd all had their fill. "I think it's time to visit the dump and see if we can find anything interesting to chew on. It's a great way to round off a good meal! Coming, Lily?"

"Well, I'd like to," replied Lily politely, "but I really must keep on looking for Jack."

The two dogs looked disappointed. "Aren't you going to join our gang?" asked Shep.

"If you don't mind, I'd rather not," said Lily. "But I'm very grateful to you both. I'll never forget your kindness."

Sam cocked his head at her. "It's a great life on the streets, you know. Freedom, independence, adventure . . ."

"But I want to be with Jack," Lily explained. "He means more to me than anything in the world."

Lily trotted on until she came to a neighborhood on the edge of town with wide, tree-lined roads. The houses were bigger than the one she had lived in with Jack. They had bigger backyards, too. Lily could see fields and woods in the distance. But she was exhausted and sat down to rest.

"Oh, look at that little puppy. She must be lost!"

Lily looked up and saw a girl about the same age as Jack. She was with her parents.

The girls came toward Lily and held her hand out. "Come here, puppy," she coaxed.

Lily shrank away at first, but she was too tired to run any more, and these people looked very kind and nice. They reminded Lily of her own family. She let her tail give a tiny wag.

"What shall we do with her?" said the girl's mother. She picked Lily up and inspected her collar. "There's no name tag or telephone number," she said.

"Can we keep her?" asked the girl excitedly.

"No, Sally," said her father. "She must belong to someone. We'd better take her to the dog pound. They'll look after her till her owners come and get her."

Lily found herself being carried into the driveway of a nearby house and placed on Sally's lap in the back seat of a big yellow car.

Sally began to pet Lily with slow, soothing strokes along her furry head and back. Lily began to feel sleepy. She gave Sally's hand a lick, then curled up, ready to have a snooze.

The car engine started. Then all of a sudden, as the car pulled out of the driveway, Lily heard a familiar sound. It was the crunching noise of Mrs. Harper's car engine, coming around the corner.

Lily's ears pricked and she sat up, wide-awake again. She jumped off Sally's lap and stood up on her back legs to peer out of the back window.

There were Jack and his mom in the red car! Jack's face was streaming with tears. They were pulling into the driveway next door!

Lily started to bark, but Jack couldn't hear her. The yellow car was gathering

speed now, taking her farther and farther away. She whined, then started to howl at the top of her voice.

"It's all right, puppy," said Sally, stroking Lily again. "Calm down. You needn't be frightened of the car."

"I'm not!" Lily barked back. "You don't understand! I've finally found Jack and now you're taking me away from him!"

Chapter Five

The blanket in Lily's cage at the dog pound smelled funny, like the stuff Jack's mom used to clean the kitchen. Lily circled around on the blanket a few times, then settled down. She was in a large, bright room full of other cages.

Lily had never seen so many dogs in her life. They were all sorts of colors, shapes, and sizes, and they barked and whined in different voices. They had all looked up when she'd been brought in, then kept on making their din.

Lily's heart felt sad and heavy. What if Jack didn't come to find her? She'd never see him again! She sighed and settled down into a fretful sleep.

"Oh, Mrs. Boyd, why did you have to leave me on my own!" whined a voice very close by.

Lily opened one eye and peered into the cage next to her. The spaniel sitting there looked very sad. "Hello, I'm Lily," she woofed.

"I'm Charlie," the spaniel replied.

"Who's Mrs. Boyd?" Lily asked.

"She was my owner," whimpered Charlie. "We were very happy. But then she was taken to the hospital and never came back. Her neighbor brought me here."

Lily's heart went out to Charlie. He was even worse off than she was! At least Lily could hope that Jack would come and get her. "Perhaps someone will come along to give you a new home," said Lily kindly.

"No they won't," replied Charlie sadly "People only want puppies. I'm two years old!"

Lily decided to try and cheer Charlie up. She started telling him all about her big adventure on the streets, and all the dogs she had met, until his sad, brown eyes began to close in sleep. . . .

By morning, the two dogs were firm friends, snuggled up on each side of the cage wall that separated them, fast asleep.

"Here she is! Lily, did you say her name was?"

At the sound of her name, Lily woke with a start and looked up. She blinked and looked again. She couldn't believe her eyes! There, in front of her cage, was

Jack! With Mrs. Harper and Sally, the girl who'd brought her here yesterday!

"Lily!" cried Jack. "I'm here! I've come to get you!"

Lily yelped with delight and sat up, wagging her tail so hard it became a blur.

A girl in a green uniform opened the cage and Lily leaped into Jack's arms, licking his face all over. She wriggled so much he nearly dropped her.

Jack was crying and laughing all at the same time, and Mrs. Harper looked a bit tearful too.

"There, Jack! I told you we'd find her!" she said in a rather wobbly voice, dabbing at her eyes with a tissue.

"What an amazing coincidence, Lil!"

said Jack. "Somehow you found our new street yesterday. And when Sally and her family came over to welcome us, they told us they'd just taken a lost puppy to the dog pound. It was you!"

Lily licked one of Jack's ears happily. "Yes," she woofed. "Amazing."

"Come on then, Lil! Let's go and show you our new home," said Jack, putting her leash on.

Lily suddenly remembered Charlie. She looked over Jack's shoulder to say goodbye to him.

"Bye, Charlie!" she barked. "Don't give up hope!"

But Charlie was busy wagging his tail and snuffling away at Sally, who had crouched down beside his cage and was talking to him in a quiet voice.

Once Lily saw her basket in the kitchen of the new house, the idea of living there didn't seem so strange after all. Jack loved his new bedroom, and his new friend, Sally, who came over often to play in their big new garden. She and her family lived next door.

Early one morning, a few days later, Lily was stopped in her tracks as she raced around the yard. She heard yapping in Sally's backyard. It sounded familiar.

She ran up to a hole in the fence and peered through. Her small black nose touched another, bigger, black nose. Lily recognized it instantly.

"Charlie!" Lily yelped in surprise. "What are you doing in Sally's yard?"

"It's my yard too, now," Charlie woofed happily. "Thanks to you, I've found a new home!"

Charlie explained that when Sally had returned from visiting the dog pound, she'd told her mom all about the spaniel she'd made friends with. She'd persuaded her parents to go and see Charlie. They'd liked him, too, and had brought him home with them.

"That's great!" yipped Lily happily. "Now *I've* got a friend next door, too!"

"Charlie, come on, let's ask Mom if

we can go next door and play with Jack and Lily," said Sally from the other side of the fence.

"See you in a minute," barked Charlie. He turned and ran over to his new owner, his long, silky ears flapping.

Lily gave a little leap of joy, then trotted off to find Jack. She was bursting with happiness.

Jack came running out to meet her. "Come on, Lil, race you to the end of the street!"

"Wait a minute!" barked Lily, her tail wagging hard. "Our friends are coming around. We can all race together!"

Puppy Friends Activity Fun Pages

Developed by Stasia Ward Kehoe

Lost Lily Trivia Quiz

1. What kind of dog is Lily?
2. What color car does Jack's mother drive?
3. What happens when Lily drinks from the puddle in the park?
4. Why does Sally's family bring Lily to the dog pound?
5. Who comes to live at Sally's house at the end of the story?

(see answers at bottom of page)

Fun Frames

Frame your favorite dog's face with this fun craft. You will need:

Eight to twelve wooden ice cream sticks
Craft glue
Pens/felt-tip markers
Colored string
Two-sided tape

Answers: 1. Jack Russell terrier 2. Red 3. It tastes awful 4. So that her family can find her there 5. Charlie, the dog Lily met at the dog pound

Arrange the wooden ice cream sticks two or three to a side to form a square frame. Glue the sticks together. Use the pen or marker to draw puppy faces or dog bones, or write your dog's name right on the frame. Loop a piece of string over the top edge of the frame for hanging your picture. Put a small square of two-sided tape in each of the four back corners of the frame and attach a picture of your pet.

Lost and Found Stories

This story describes Lily's feelings when she was left alone, lost, and found. Try writing your own lost-and-found story. Perhaps you were once lost. Maybe you once lost a pet or favorite toy. Write about this experience, or use your imagination to invent a story. Have your story answer these four questions: How did you (or your pet or toy) get lost? How did you feel when you were lost? How were you found? How did you feel when you were found? Write the words of the story on three to five sheets of paper, making sure to leave space to draw pictures. Make a cover for your story from a piece of construction paper. Write the title, and "Written and illustrated by YOUR NAME" on the cover. Stack the completed pages of your story in order, lay the cover on top, and staple along one side to create your very own book.

Paw Print Stamp

Take a close look at the bottom of your puppy's paws. Notice the one large central foot pad and four smaller foot pads that surround it. Now you are ready to make a paw-print stamp. *Ask an adult for help, and gather the following items:*

   1 oval baking potato
Plastic knife, baby spoon, or other carving utensil
Paper towels
Pencil
Acrylic paints
1 paper plate
Newsprint or large sheets of white paper

Cut the potato in half, crosswise. Rinse both halves in cool water and pat dry. With the pencil, roughly sketch or scratch the outline of a paw print on the flat side of one potato half. Use the plastic knife or baby spoon to scrape away all the potato around the paw shape until the paw print is slightly raised above the rest of the potato. Pour a little paint on the paper plate. Lightly dip your potato stamp in the paint, then press onto the paper and lift. You will see a brightly colored paw print. Cover the paper with colorful paw prints. Carve the other potato half into a dog bone stamp or other shape and print away. [Hint: This makes great homemade wrapping paper.]

Wagging Word Search

Can you think of fourteen different things dogs do? See if you can find them in the word search below. Try looking in columns, rows, and on diagonals. The first one is circled to show you how.

(see answers below)

```
W J N E M L S N I F F K E
B A R K N V B B M K L M S
E S G K X J T R U K C I N
Q I O T M C H B A A D K U
I E P O A Y O F M C V J G
Y R U O F I W S F I E M G
W P R Q G V L Q C H C E L
G L J A I E O I B O I U E
M A F K M Y I P F H R W J
B Y C R W X P H P W C E M
L I R G W O O F Z W L C M
L R U I H F U I A O E C E
A Y N Q W P O U M J O H U
F L K F G R O W L H G J C
```

Puppy Care Pointers

"The Name Game"

Lily had a hard time getting home to her family because she did not have a name tag on her collar. Check that your pet's collar carries a tag with her name and a way to reach her owner. Be sure to follow your city or town's leash and licensing rules. Then you can feel certain that if your dog does get lost, she'll soon be found.

"Big Changes for Little Puppies"

Whenever changes happen—a move to a new house, the arrival of a new family member or pet, even a home improvement project—puppies need care and reassurance. Consider what special attention your puppy will need to adjust to the change. Keep up as many usual routines, such as walk times, feeding times, and sleeping location, as possible. Watch carefully for any changes in your pet's mood or behavior—these may be warning signs that your pet may need even more help adjusting to the change than you do!

Coming soon . . .

Spot the Sporty Puppy

Suddenly Spot saw Matt. He was dressed in his gym clothes and was standing on the opposite side of the track. Spot was so excited he dashed out from under the chair where he was hiding and across the track. At exactly the same moment, the teachers came running at full speed toward him, with Mr. Brown in the lead.

Spot had no time to get out of the way. Neither did the principal!